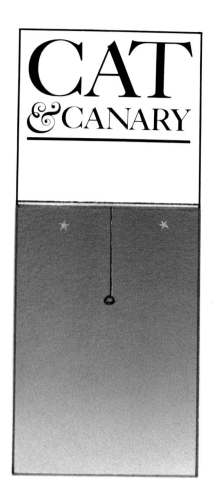

CAT
&CANARY

This paperback edition first published in 2003 by Andersen Press Ltd.
The rights of Michael Foreman to be identified as the author and illustrator of this work
have been asserted by him in accordance with the Copyright, Designs and Patents Act, 1988.
First published in Great Britain in 1984 by Andersen Press Ltd. 20 Vauxhall Bridge Road, London SW1V 2SA.
Published in Australia by Random House Australia Pty., 20 Alfred Street, Milsons Point, Sydney, NSW 2061.
Printed and bound in Italy by Grafiche AZ, Verona.

10 9 8 7 6 5 4 3 2 1

British Library Cataloguing in Publication Data available.

ISBN 1 84270 287 4

This book has been printed on acid-free paper

CAT
& CANARY
MICHAEL FOREMAN

Andersen Press London

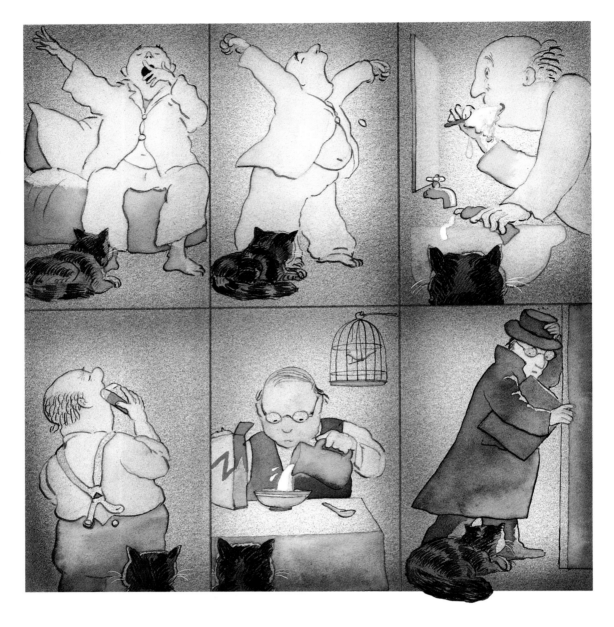

It was dawn in the city. Cat watched the winter sky change from night to day. Canary was still asleep in her cage.

Every day Cat watched his master get out of bed, clean his teeth, and eat his breakfast.

Every day the man would say, "Oh, you are lucky. You just lie around the house all day, lazy cat." Then he put on his hat and coat and went to work.

But every day, as soon as the man had left, Cat let Canary out of her cage. The bird always flew around the room a few times, and then they had breakfast together.

After breakfast they went up to the roof. Canary would fly high and dive and whirl about in the sky.

Cat wished he could fly with his friend above the streets and bridges to the land beyond the river.

Cat often watched other cats on other roofs chasing birds.

He never chased birds. After all, his best friend was a canary.

All the birds flocked to his roof. He loved their colour and he loved their song.

Why should he chase them away just because he was a cat?

One windy day Cat found a kite tangled around
a television aerial. He freed the kite, but
became tangled in the string. The wind blew
the kite and the kite whisked Cat up into the
air and over the streets far below.

The cats on the other roofs were amazed to see Cat flying. "Come down!" they yelled. "Flying is for the birds."

Winds rushing between the high buildings blew him higher until he was flying amongst the very tallest skyscrapers.

Canary tried desperately to keep up with him, but Cat
was being blown further and further away.

After the first terrible fright, Cat was thrilled to be flying
free as a bird.

His wish had come true.

He had a bird's-eye view of the city and the shining river.

The sun turned the great buildings to gold and silver
and threw the giant shadow of Cat across surprised people
far below.

But soon the sun was covered by storm clouds
and Cat no longer felt free as a bird.

The huge buildings now looked dangerous and threatening.

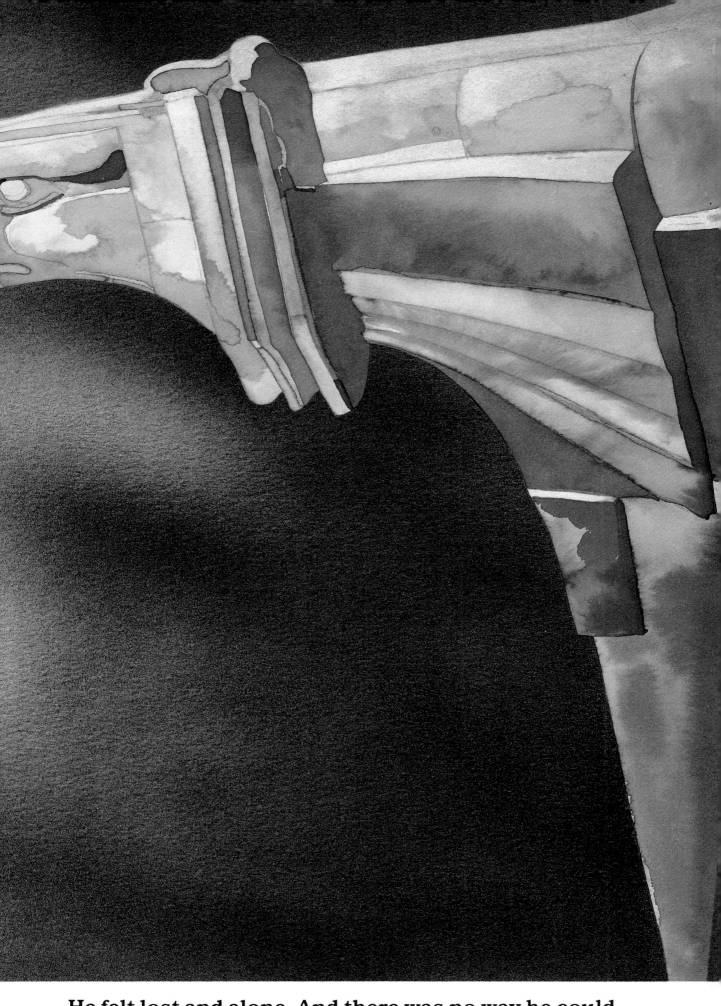

He felt lost and alone. And there was no way he could control the kite.

He was being blown further and further from home.

Below he could see the icy river. Snow began to fall.

Suddenly, through the tumbling snowflakes, appeared Canary with a large flock of birds. The birds took the tail of the kite and the string and turned for home. Cat was no longer alone.

Down they went, through the snow towards

the bright flashing lights of the city.

They landed back on their roof just as their master turned the corner of the street. The man did not see them. His head was bent against the wind, and snow blew into his face and down his neck. "Oh to be a cat," he thought, "and stay home in the warm and do nothing."

Cat waved a paw to the birds, and tied the kite to the
television aerial ready for the next day.

Then Cat and Canary raced downstairs, and when the master opened the door, Canary was swinging in the cage and Cat was curled up on the mat with his eyes closed.

"What a lazy cat! I bet you haven't moved all day."

Cat opened one eye, and then closed it again.

"Tomorrow,"
he thought,
"if we all fly together,
we can go to the land
beyond the river.
And still be back for tea."